WHO'S A PEST?

WHO'S A PEST?

An **I CAN READ** Book

by CROSBY NEWELL BONSALL

HARPER & ROW, PUBLISHERS
NEW YORK, EVANSTON
AND LONDON

WHO'S A PEST?

Copyright © 1962 by Crosby Newell Bonsall
Printed in the United States of America

Library of Congress catalog card number: 62–13310

To Plunketts Creek
with love

Lolly, Molly, Polly, and Dolly
all looked at Homer.
Homer was their brother.

6

"I didn't do it," said Homer.

"Yes, you did," they said.

"Yes, you did. And you're a pest!"

Then Lolly and Molly and Polly
and Dolly all turned their backs.
"Beans," said Homer,
"I'm not a pest."
But Lolly, Molly, Polly,
and Dolly walked away.

8

Down by the woodpile

Homer said again,

"I'm not a pest!"

"I never said you were,"

said a lizard.

"I never said you said I was,"
said Homer.

"I never said you said I said
you were," said the lizard.

"I never said you said I said
you said I was," said Homer.

"Said what?" asked the lizard.

"Said I was a pest," said Homer.

"Who?" asked the lizard.

"You," said Homer.

"Me?" said the lizard,

"I'm no pest."

11

"I never said you were," said Homer.

"I never said you said I was,"

said the lizard.

"Beans," said Homer.

"You started it," said the lizard.

"You are a pest!"

And the lizard slipped away.

"Beans," said Homer,

"I'm not a pest."

He ran all the way

down a hill

and met a chipmunk.

13

"What time is it?"

asked the chipmunk.

"Ten to two," said Homer.

"Ten to who?" asked the chipmunk.

"Not who—what," said Homer.

"Ten to what?" asked the chipmunk.

"Yes," said Homer.

"YES," cried the chipmunk,

"what kind of time is that?"

"It isn't the time," Homer said.

"But I asked for the time,"

said the chipmunk.

"I told you," said Homer.

"What?" asked the chipmunk.

"The time," said Homer.

"What time?" asked the chipmunk.

"The time it was then," said Homer.

"When was then?" asked the chipmunk.

"Then was when you asked me,"
said Homer.

"When did I ask you?"

asked the chipmunk.

"At ten to two," said Homer.

"But that was then,"

said the chipmunk.

"What time is it now?"

"Two to two," said Homer.

"Don't toot at me,"

said the chipmunk.

"You're a pest!"

And the chipmunk ran away.

"Beans," said Homer,

"I'm not a pest!"

"No one ever thinks he's a pest,"

said a rabbit.

"You can't tell about yourself."

"I can tell about myself," said Homer.

"*They* can't tell about myself."

"About me," said the rabbit.

"You?" asked Homer.

"They can't tell about *me*,"

said the rabbit.

"You, too?" asked Homer.

"No, you," said the rabbit.

"They can't tell about *you*."

20

"That's what I said," said Homer.

"Now what shall I do?"

"I'm glad you asked me,"

said the rabbit. "I'm not a pest,

so I shall be able to tell you

how *not* to be a pest."

"Okay," said Homer.

"Stay out of gardens,"
said the rabbit.

"But I don't go into gardens,"
Homer said.

"Well, stay out of them, anyway,"
said the rabbit.

"But if I'm not in,
how can I stay out?" Homer asked.

"It's easy," said the rabbit.

"You can stay out by not going in."

"But I *am* out," Homer said.

"You're lucky," said the rabbit,

"you got out in time."

"But I was never in," said Homer.

"Oh, hush," said the rabbit,

"the others were right.

You *are* a pest!"

And the rabbit hopped away.

"Beans," said Homer,

"I'm not a pest!"

Homer sat down.

Soon he heard a sound.

"Help," it said.

"Help! Help! Help!"

Homer looked around.

"Help who?" he asked.

"Help me," said the sound.

"Who's me?" Homer asked.

"Me is me. I don't know

who *you* are," said the sound.

"I'm Homer," said Homer.

"Please help me, Homer,"

said the sound.

"Where are you?" cried Homer.

"Here," said the sound.

"Where's here?" asked Homer.

"Here is here," said the sound.

"Oh, my," cried Homer,

"I'll never find you.

I don't know where here is."

"Then find someone who does,"

cried the sound.

Just then the rabbit came along.

"You must help me," Homer cried.

"Oh, it's you," said the rabbit.

"What a pest!"

"Me is lost," Homer cried.

"You don't look lost to me,"
said the rabbit.

"I'm not lost," Homer said,
"Me is."

"Who is Me?" asked the rabbit.

"You are the rabbit," Homer said.

"I know that," snapped the rabbit.

"Who is the Me you're talking about?"

"He says he is Me," Homer said.

"Well, if he says he is you,"

said the rabbit, "we must find you.

And here you are!"

31

The chipmunk ran by and stopped.

"Please help us," Homer said.

"Oh, it's you," said the chipmunk.

"What a pest!"

"He wants us to find Me,"

said the rabbit.

"Find you?" said the chipmunk.

"You are here!"

"No, no," cried the rabbit,

"Me is here."

"That's what I said,"

cried the chipmunk.

"What did you say?" asked the lizard.

He slipped from behind a tree.

"He said he was here," Homer said.

"Oh, it's you," said the lizard.

"What a pest!

Who's here?" he asked.

"Me," said the rabbit.

"HELP!" said the sound.

"What is that?" cried the rabbit

and the chipmunk

and the lizard.

"That is Me," said Homer.

"You!" they cried.

"No, ME," cried the sound.

"I'm here."

Lolly and Molly and Polly

and Dolly skipped by.

They saw Homer. "Oh, it's you,"

they said. "What a pest!"

But Homer didn't hear.

He and the rabbit and the chipmunk

and the lizard were looking all over.

"What are you looking for?" asked

Lolly, Molly, Polly, and Dolly.

"Not what, who," Homer said.

"Not who, whom," said the rabbit.

"Whom what?" asked the girls.

"Whom are you looking for?"

said the chipmunk.

"We're not looking for anyone,"
said Lolly, Molly, Polly,
and Dolly.
"Well, start looking for ME,"
said the sound.

Lolly took a step back.

Crash!

Lolly wasn't there anymore.

Molly went to look.

Crash!

Molly wasn't there anymore.

39

Polly ran over.

Crash!

Polly wasn't there anymore.

Dolly ran after Polly.

Crash!

Dolly wasn't there anymore.

"This is silly,"

said the rabbit. He hopped over.

Crash!

The rabbit wasn't there anymore.

The chipmunk went after him.

Crash!

The chipmunk wasn't there anymore.

"Well," said the lizard,

"it's my turn now."

Crash!

The lizard wasn't there anymore.

"HELP!" cried the sound.

"Help! Help! Help! Help!"

cried Lolly, Molly, Polly,

and Dolly.

"Help!" cried the rabbit

and the chipmunk

and the lizard.

"I think I'll go home," said Homer.

But if he went home without

his sisters, his mother would say,

"Well, Homer, where are your sisters?

Where are Lolly and Molly and Polly

and Dolly?"

And Homer would say, "In a hole."

And think of the lizard.

And all the little lizards

waiting for their father.

And their father was in a hole.

And think of the chipmunk.

And all the little chipmunks

waiting for their father.

And their father was in a hole.

And think of the rabbit.

And all the little rabbits

waiting for their father.

And their father was in a hole.

And think of the sound,

whatever it was.

And all the little whatevers

waiting for their father.

And their father was in a hole.

So Homer got them all out.

How? Easy as pie.

This is what he told them:

"Lizard, sit on the chipmunk.

Chipmunk, sit on the rabbit.

Rabbit, sit on Lolly.

Lolly, sit on Molly.

Molly, sit on Polly.

Polly, sit on Dolly.

Dolly, sit on whatever it is

making the sound."

And then—

Homer pulled the lizard

who pulled the chipmunk

who pulled the rabbit

who pulled Lolly

and Molly

and Polly

and Dolly

who pulled

and pulled

whatever it was.

What was it?

It was a bear.

"I'm a pest," he said.

"No! No! No! No!" said Lolly
and Molly and Polly and Dolly.
"No!" said the lizard
and the chipmunk.
"No, indeed," said the rabbit,
"there's the pest," and he
looked at Homer.

"Not at all," said the bear.

"He got me out."

"He did not, I did,"

snapped the rabbit.

"You did not, I did,"

cried the chipmunk.

"You are both wrong, I did,"

said the lizard.

"No, we did," cried Lolly and Molly

and Polly and Dolly.

"I don't see how," said the bear.

"You were all in the hole with me."

"Oh," said the rabbit.

"Mmmm," said the chipmunk.

"Uh," said the lizard.

Lolly looked at the sky.

Molly looked at her toes.

Polly looked at her nails.

And Dolly rubbed her nose.

57

"Now," said the bear,

"I fell in a hole.

I made a lot of fuss

so—that makes me a pest.

You each fell in the hole.

You each made a lot of fuss.

So—that makes each of you

a pest!"

The bear looked at Homer.

"There is just one

who is not a pest."

"Who is that?" asked Homer.

"Well, if you don't know,"

snapped the rabbit.

"We won't tell you," cried

the chipmunk.

"Right," said the lizard.

"What a pest!"

"Beans," said Homer.

"I'm not a pest!"

"Right! Right! Right! Right!"

sang Lolly, Molly, Polly,

and Dolly.

"That's what *I* said," said the lizard.

"Said what?" asked the rabbit.

"Said who?" asked the chipmunk.

"I didn't say anything,"
said the bear.

"We didn't say you did,"
said Lolly and Molly and Polly
and Dolly.

"I didn't say you said I did,"

said the lizard.

"Yes, you did," said the rabbit.

"You keep out of this," snapped

the chipmunk. "You're a pest!"

Homer and the bear walked away.

"You see how it is," said the bear.

"I see how it is," said Homer.

He looked back.

"Hey," he yelled,

"YOU'RE ALL PESTS!"

Then Homer and the bear

ran off over the hill.